IN THE NEXT THREE SECONDS

by Rowland Morgan

illustrated by Rod and Kira Josey

PUFFIN BOOKS

PUFFIN BOOKS
Published by the Penguin Group
Penguin Putnam Books for Young Readers, 345 Hudson Street, New York, New York 10014, U.S.A.
Penguin Books Ltd, 27 Wrights Lane, London W8 5TZ, England
Penguin Books Australia Ltd, Ringwood, Victoria, Australia
Penguin Books Canada Ltd, 10 Alcorn Avenue, Toronto, Ontario, Canada M4V 3B2
Penguin Books (N.Z.) Ltd, 182-190 Wairau Road, Auckland 10, New Zealand

Penguin Books Ltd, Registered Offices: Harmondsworth, Middlesex, England

First published in the United States of America by Lodestar Books,
an affiliate of Dutton Children's Books, a division of Penguin Books USA Inc., 1997
Published in Great Britain by Hamlyn Children's books, an imprint of Reed Consumer Books Ltd., 1997
Published by Puffin Books, a member of Penguin Putnam Books for Young Readers, 1999

1 3 5 7 9 10 8 6 4 2

THE LIBRARY OF CONGRESS HAS CATALOGED THE LODESTAR EDITION AS FOLLOWS:
Morgan, Rowland.
In the next three seconds / by Rowland Morgan;
illustrated by Rod and Kira Josey.—1st American ed.
p. cm.
Includes index.
Summary: Predicts events that will occur in the near and distant future, including
"In the next three months, 1,000 households in Zimbabwe will be hooked up to solar electricity."
ISBN 0-525-67551-5 (alk. paper)
1. Forecasting—Juvenile literature. [1. Forecasting.]
I. Josey, Rod, ill. II. Josey, Kira, ill. III. Title.
CB 161.M669 1997 96-38480 CIP AC
303.49'09'05—dc20

Puffin Books ISBN 0-14-056624-4

Printed in Spain

CONTENTS

INTRODUCTION

Throughout human history, people have been measuring all kinds of things.

Counting was probably done by caterers for imperial banquets in ancient China. If they didn't plan enough food for the emperor's guests, he'd see that their heads were chopped off. They planned ahead by counting and measuring, using beads on strings in a frame, a tool called an abacus.

Now people use a whole toolchest of equipment for measuring: stopwatches, clocks, timers, calculators, gauges, scales, balances, yardsticks, monitors, probes, and of course, computers. Computers have compiled enormous hoards of information about everything under the sun.

Practically every move we make is noted somewhere by an electronic brain—even issuing textbooks at school and buying candy at the corner store. People feed information into computers about almost everything, from the movements of microbes to the deeds of dinosaurs. The facts in this book are worked out from this great new wealth of information.

Now, in the next three minutes, how much of this book will you read?

HOW TO MAKE YOUR OWN PREDICTIONS

First, choose a fact about the past that you find interesting. Lots of interesting statistics are quoted on TV, in newspapers, or in schoolbooks, supplying you with measures of the past. Then find some conclusions you can draw by working out how this fact can be turned into an average measurement of some kind. For example: Bottled water factories told a marketing firm conducting a sales survey that they sold eight quarts of mineral water per Briton in a recent year. How much mineral water will Britons use in the next three days?

First, multiply the number of Britons by the quarts of packaged
water they use:

58,000,000 x 8 = 464 million

Then divide that total by the number of days in a year:

464,000,000 ÷ 365 = 1,271,233 quarts a day

To find three days, multiply by three:

1,271,233 x 3 = 3,813,699 quarts

There is your prediction: In the next three days, Britons
will chug nearly 3.8 million quarts of mineral water. Now
try expressing that rather long number in a way that is easier to imagine.
For example: a typical bathtub holds 159 quarts. So work out the number
of bathtubs of mineral water Britons will use in the next three days like this:

3,813,699 ÷ 159 = 23,986 bathtubfuls

Perhaps it is still hard to imagine so many bathtubs of water, so how about another conversion?
A large tanker truck carries approximately 34,000 quarts, so work out your prediction in
tanker trucks, as follows:

3,813,699 ÷ 34,000 = 112 tanker trucks

If you still think it is hard to picture so many tanker trucks, why not line them up?
A tanker truck is 49 feet long. Allow two feet parking distance at each end,
bringing the total length to 51 feet, and make the following calculation:

112 x 51 = 5,712 ft or 1.08 mi

So your prediction becomes: In the next three days,
Britons will drink enough mineral water to fill a
line of large trucks one mile long!

Here are some useful figures for making conversions:

Bathtub .... 160 quarts
Semitrailer truck .... 28 tons (49 feet long)
Semitrailer tanker truck .... 34,000 quarts
Supertanker ship .... 110,000 tons
Olympic swimming pool .... 2.40 million quarts
Tarbela Dam (world's biggest) .... weighs 267 million tons
Airliner fuel consumption .... 13 gallons per mile
Tennis court .... 316 sq yards
Soccer field .... 2.47 acres
Toaster .... 800 watts

IN THE NEXT THREE SECONDS...

The planet Earth will orbit 56 miles around the sun.

Your heart will beat nearly three tim...

Japanese eaters will throw away two pairs of CHOPSTICKS made from felled Malaysian rain forests.

The human population will increase by NINE.

Motor Vehicles will use three tanker trucks of gasoline.

Americans will buy 56 air-conditioning units.

RUSSIANS WILL MAIL MORE THAN 4,000 LETTERS OR PARCELS.

MAGICAL MYSTERY TOUR

Enough tourists to FILL a bus will arrive SOMEWHERE.

A sei whale could dive 170 feet at the speed of a Naval submarine.

A CRUISING Boeing 757 airliner will burn three cupfuls of KEROSENE in the arid upper atmosphere.

LOGGERS will cut down 799 trees.

93 trees will be cut down to make the liners for disposable diapers.

CHINESE PEOPLE WILL BUY THREE COLOR TVs.

A TGV express train in FRANCE will travel the length of eight tennis courts.

Britons will CONSUME a stack of 1lb cans of baked beans four times as high as St. Paul's Cathedral.

Italians will DRINK a stack of cases of mineral water, as HIGH as the Statue of Liberty.

AMERICANS will eat 6,000 eggs.

95 AIRLINERS WILL TAKE OFF.

106 children around the world will receive a vaccination.

Three teddy bears will be given as gifts.

A flying midge (genus Forcipomyia) will beat its wings 3,100 times.

Irish people will drink 200 potfuls of tea.

Four new MOTOR vehicles will be driven out of FACTORIES.

Americans will buy eight dishwashers.

A Sprinting Cheetah will cover three-quarters... the length of a soccer field.

18 years' worth of TELEVISION will be watched by people around the world.

The place where you are now on Earth will revolve 0.87 mile eastward.

Italians will kill ten songbirds for bite-sized morsels.

Americans will throw away 3,000 aluminum beverage cans.

US Cola 50¢

The holder of the WORLD LAND speed record could pass 212 parked cars.

RODENTS WILL EAT ENOUGH TO FEED 19 STARVING PEOPLE.

Fijians will pick 38 coconuts.

Britons will eat 3,600 potatoes.

11 tourists will arrive in France.

Saskatchewan farmers will produce 22 tons of wheat, enough for **200,000** loaves.

An animated cartoon will use 4,320 pictures.

IN THE NEXT THREE MINUTES...

People on Earth will eat the weight of 100 great blue whales (14,000 tons of food).

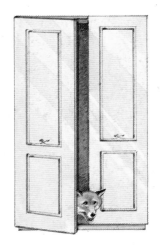

A wild fox will be trapped and skinned by Canadian furriers.

British doctors will write 750 prescriptions for Asthma.

One baby will be born to an unmarried mother in Britain.

A pelican will catch and eat half an ounce of fish.

People on Earth will take six railcars of aspirin.

Germans will buy a stack of personal stereos almost seven feet HIGH.

French people will save 600 trees by recycling paper.

Drivers will travel far enough on Western European motorways to go around the world 45 times.

You will secrete 0.07 fluid ounce of saliva.

French women will buy 1.7 tons of bath soap.

World farmers will spread 1,500 tons of chemical fertilizers.

Chinese builders will pour six semi-trailer truck loads of concrete for the 20-year Three Gorges dam project on the Yangtze River.

Americans will buy a stack of new major electrical appliances as tall as one of the world's tallest buildings, the Sears Tower, Chicago.

Enough razors will be junked by western Europeans to follow the white line along the

Calais to Geneva road (480 mi).

The Super Nintendo console will recognize 10,588 different signals from the official control pad.

Fishermen will kill more than 23 wild porpoises or dolphins.

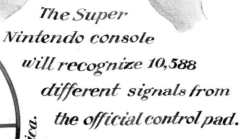

People will buy 176 mobile phones.

A poacher will kill a wild elephant in central Africa.

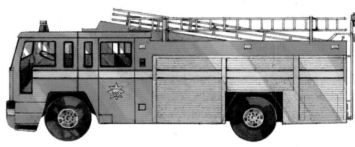

British fire companies will put out 2.4 fires.

A Dromiceiomimus dinosaur (Late Cretaceous period from Alberta, Canada) could have sprinted 2 miles.

British dairy cows will give 84 pails of cream (26-gallon pail).

Children in 1.5 British families will see their parents divorce.

Europe's shops will receive enough throwaway aerosol cans to fill more than three miles of shelving.

Americans will eat four and a half head of cattle as take-out hamburgers.

Germans will buy one stack of 119 color TVs more than two times as high as the walls of the Kremlin palace in MOSCOW.

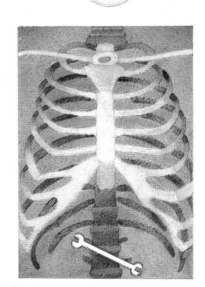

British public-service surgeons will perform 24 free-of-charge operations.

17 species of life will disappear from the tropical rain forests.

IN THE NEXT THREE HOURS...

Certain types of bamboo will grow 9.0 in. when exposed to the

MENU -
Americans will eat 600,000 lobsters.

Americans will buy 4,500 pairs of jeans.

Sewage the weight of 80 Paris Arcs de Triomphe will be pumped into the harbor of Boston.

Meteosat, the weather satellite, will take six complete pictures of the clouds over Europe, Africa, and the Atlantic Ocean.

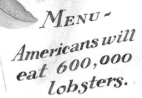

One ton of the planet's living coral will be broken off reefs for sale in souvenir shops.

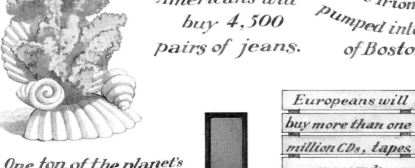

Europeans will buy more than one million CDs, tapes, or records.

Oil-rich Middle Eastern states will spend about $15 million on machinery for war.

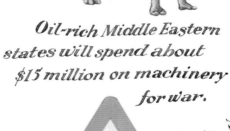

A butterfly will transform from a pupa into a beautiful, fluttering adult.

Children will lose 11 hairs from their head, and these will be replaced (old folks lose 15 permanently).

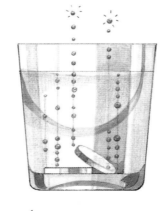

Americans will spend more than $1 million on remedies for indigestion.

More than 3,000 wild animals will be killed on Europe's roads.

Four bullet trains of people will

be added to crowded Japan's population.

Americans will use paper that requires 375,000 trees to make.

More than 500 baby rabbits will be adopted as family pets.

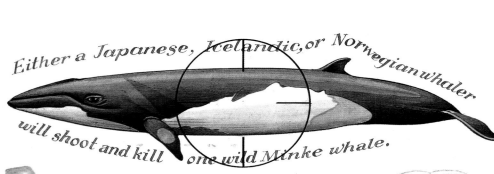

Either a Japanese, Icelandic, or Norwegian whaler will shoot and kill one wild Minke whale.

Five airplanes will pass over the British Isles carrying radioactive materials.

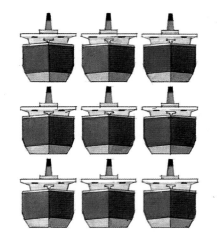

It's for you-hoo!

French people will spend $2 million on perfume.

American smokers will THROW away a (horizontally-laid) stack of 350,000 cigarette lighters as high as Oregon's Mount Hood.

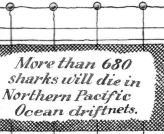

More than 680 sharks will die in Northern Pacific Ocean driftnets.

Germans will buy 20 stacks of dishwashers as high as the world's tallest totem pole at Alert Bay, B.C., Canada.

Nine OIL tankers will dock in British ports.

Hardwood for 1,920 doors will be imported to Britain from tropical countries.

Italians will buy enough pairs of shoes to give everybody in Venice five pairs each.

Americans will throw away 99 miles of plastic pens.

BRITISH CATS & DOGS WILL BE FED ENOUGH PET FOOD TO FILL 1.2 MILLION CANS.

Americans will buy one STACK of telephones four times as high as Toronto's CN communications tower.

IN THE NEXT THREE DAYS...

Two inmates will escape from a British Prison.

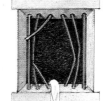

Britons will FLUSH away enough (456,000mi) toilet paper to stretch to the MOON... and back.

Enough garbage to load two WORLD FLEETS of super-TANKERS will be dumped.

Enough aluminum will be thrown away

More than 1,000,000 new bicycles will be wheeled out of factories.

DOCTOR'S NOTE:

Your cold virus will multiply itself 10,000 million times before causing your first sneeze.

Four British children under the age of three will have to be treated for a dogbite .....

A ton of wood in a forest will release a ton of oxygen.

A blue shark in a hurry could travel 1,600 miles, or from Africa .... to India.

A koala bear might well sleep for 66 hours.

DO NOT DISTURB

A rickshaw puller in Calcutta, India will earn $3.

JOURNEY INTO SPACE

Western Europeans will smoke 460 pick-up trucks of cured tobacco.

North Americans will truck enough sand and gravel (14 million tons) to make concrete for more than 1,200 New York World Trade Centers.

Enough writing will move on the computer Internet to make a stack of THICK paperback books reaching into outer space (37miles).

More than 2,™™™ products will be trade-marked in the U.S.A.

to build 63 BOEING B-52 Bombers.

More than 2,000 people OR half-mile bumper-to-bumper busloads of people will move to Florida.

People in chilly Finland will BUY a stack of cartons of ice cream two times as high as Mount Everest.

A Panda could eat a load of bamboo as heavy as the luggage FOUR passengers are allowed to have on a plane (240 lb).

TALLAHASSEE JACKSONVILLE
WELCOME TO
ORLANDO
TAMPA
FLORIDA
MIAMI
THE SUNSHINE STATE

North Americans will mine enough gold (3.5t) to make a gold necklace for each of 235,000 people.

66 Eiffel Towers.

More than two quarts of beer will be consumed per German man.

MEMO
Enough paper to cover one tennis court will be used per office worker.
Signed Weena

French women will use a bathing-pool FULL of shampoo.

Six Sri Lankans will receive a fatal snake bite (Snakes responsible: Common Krait, Cobra and Russell's viper).

Germans will make enough steel for

FRENCH pet dogs will eat the weight of a herd of 700 African elephants in pet food.

WOOF

100 species of life will be lost to deforestation.

13

About 250 million Motor vehicles...

In The Next Three Nights...

More than 80 UFO sightings will be reported around the WORLD.

OVER 15 MILLION DOLLARS WILL BE SPENT ON ADVERTISING FUEL-WASTING CARS TO AMERICANS.

$15

Somalians will give their nanny goats about 45 million dawn milkings.

150 jumbo jet loads of people will starve to death.

Three MILLION babies will be conceived.

Distribution staff of the YOMIURI SHIMBUN will send 26 million copies of the newspaper across Japan.

MEXICO

450,000 tourists will spend a night in Mexico.

The American post office will send more than 740 million pieces of first class mail: ...nearly half the world total.

12,000 Americans will brush their teeth with a newly-purchased ELECTRIC TOOTHBRUSH.

850 Australians will fly to SETTLE in crowded Britain.....

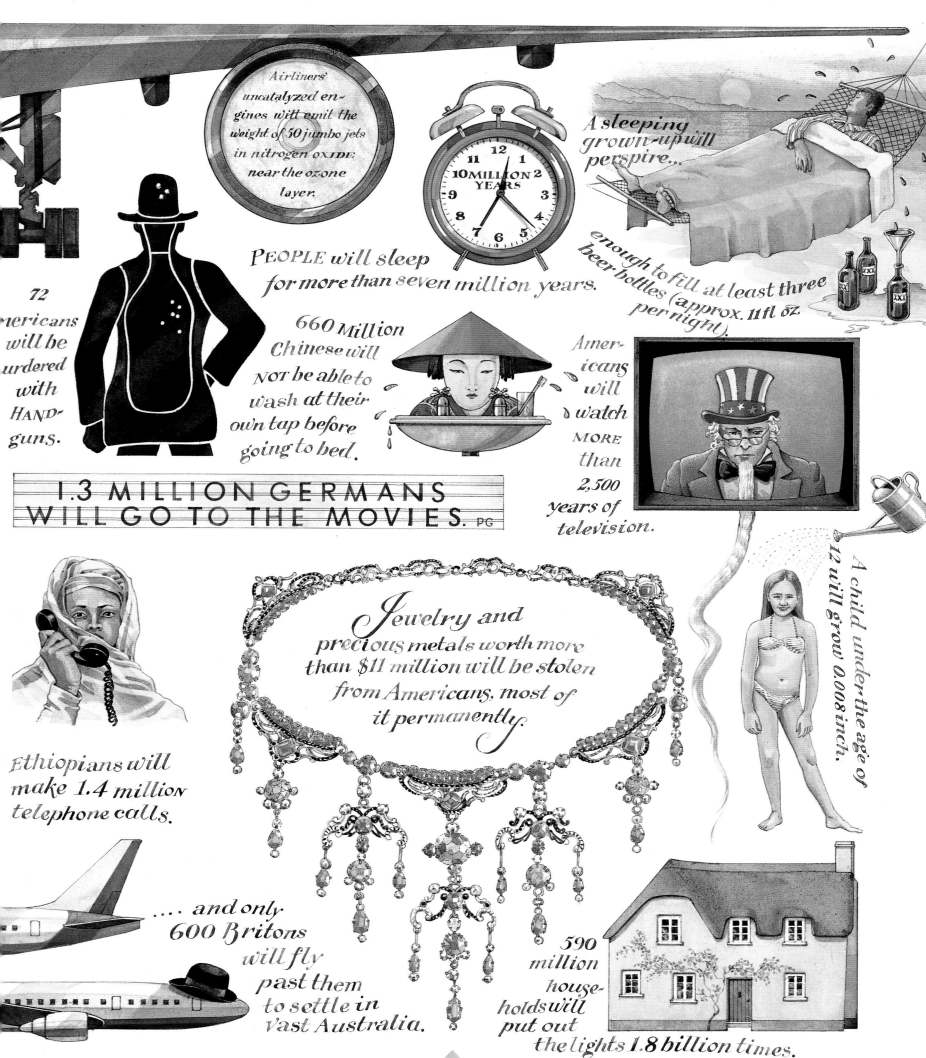

will be parked.

Airliners' uncatalyzed engines will emit the weight of 50 jumbo jets in nitrogen OXIDE near the ozone layer.

10 MILLION YEARS

PEOPLE will sleep for more than seven million years.

A sleeping grown-up will perspire... enough to fill at least three beer-bottles (approx. 11 fl. oz. per night).

72 Americans will be murdered with HAND-guns.

660 Million Chinese will NOT be able to wash at their own tap before going to bed.

Americans will watch MORE than 2,500 years of television.

1.3 MILLION GERMANS WILL GO TO THE MOVIES. PG

Jewelry and precious metals worth more than $11 million will be stolen from Americans, most of it permanently.

A child under the age of 12 will grow 0.008 inch.

Ethiopians will make 1.4 million telephone calls.

.... and only 600 Britons will fly past them to settle in vast Australia.

590 million house-holds will put out the lights 1.8 billion times.

15

345 POP songs will be released as singles in the U.K.

An American child could view more than 1,000 acts of violence on television.

200 square mi of solar furnaces in the Sahara Desert working at 10% efficiency could supply all the world's electricity.

Americans will eat 80 pizzas as BIG as the White House grounds.

·073

The leaning tower of PISA will move another 0.0028 inch off vertical.

France will spend the value of 725 Mona Lisas subsidizing Art & Culture.

More than 12,000 western European women will be caught shoplifting.

141 pedigreed Rottweilers will be registered by British dog lovers.

GRRR!

20 cyclists will be killed in Shanghai traffic.

Diplomats of Her Majesty the Q[...] a stack of SIX-packs of champa[...]

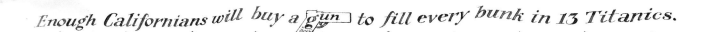

FIVE satellite launching rockets will tear a hole in the Earth's protec- tive ozone layer.

6,575 sightseers will take a flight over the Grand Canyon.

132,000 people will visit the Tower of London.

The cars of 90,000 world drivers will go permanently MISS-ING.

134 Doctors will emi- grate to Israel.

British TAXpayers will spend $260,000 on solar-power research (and $12 million on nuclear-power research).

Three people will be KILLED or wounded in a fight in Los Angeles County, home of Holly- wood.

The young herb Puya Raimondii will move one- thirteen- hundredth nearer the flowering of its only panicle in at least 80 years' time.

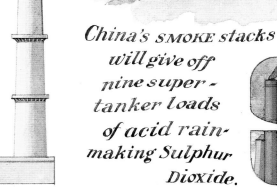
HOLLYWOOD

China's SMOKE stacks will give off nine super- tanker loads of acid rain- making Sulphur Dioxide.

SO_2

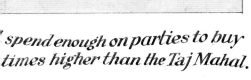
spend enough on parties to buy times higher than the Taj Mahal.

IN THE NEXT THREE MONTHS...

500 new CD-ROMs will be published for multimedia computers.

Europeans will junk a stack of cans three times (63,200 mi) higher than a (geostationary) weather satellite.

American offices will use 194 billion pieces of paper, enough to make 4,000 STACKS higher than Mount Kanchenjunga (28,210ft), (21,700 miles high).

Four million TV video game machines will be sold worldwide.

70 endangered Florida black bears will be lethally hit by road traffic.

1,000 households in Zimbabwe will be hooked up to solar electricity.

WESTERN EUROPEAN DRIVERS WILL DUMP ENOUGH METAL **OIL** FILTERS FROM THEIR ENGINES TO BUILD **7 EIFFEL TOWERS.**

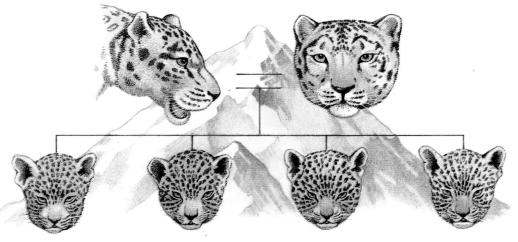

At least one extra family of baby snow leopards will be born in new game parks established around Mt. Everest in Nepal.

More than 12 million personal computers will be sold worldwide, one for each European Union child age 5-15.

An uncatalyzed car using leaded fuel and doing average mileage will emit LEAD weighing more than two soft-drink cans (2.4 ounces).

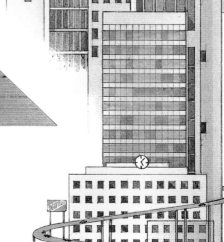

45 million households, two times the number in Britain, will be added to the world television audience.

Countries will sign 43 NEW International environmental treaties.

The U.S.A. and Russia will dismantle 1,290 nuclear BOMBS (or warheads).

80 million more people will be added to those living in world cities.

500 cinema feature films will be produced...more than a solid month of round-the-clock screening time.

Enough soybeans will be grown to outweigh seven Great Pyramids of Cheops.

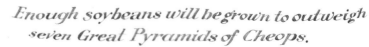

IN THE NEXT THREE YEARS...

The average American's lifestyle will require the equivalent of 5,400 buckets of coal, the average Nigerian's, 100 (30 tons, 0.6 ton).

More than 120,000 Amazon parrots will be carried overseas and sold as pets.

As part of a consumer society, your lifestyle will account for about five hot-air balloons of climate-changing carbon dioxide being emitted.

One England-size area of Siberian pine-forest will be cleared (50,000 sq mi).

Enough cars will be added to the world fleet to clog

12,000 miles

of six-lane highway.

100,000 new midsize Buick cars will be SOLD for the first time to Chinese communists.

One rat could have

2 0, 0 0 0, 0 0 0 DESCENDANTS.

Enough tourists will take a holiday on the Mediterranean coast to empty the rest of western Europe.

The traditional British landscape will lose enough hedgerows to girdle the world.

The British will use enough water to drain Loch Ness and reveal...

the monster!

75 people will be added to 0.4 square mile of Bangladesh.

Human settlements will emit enough climate~changing carbon dioxide to fill two chains of Hindenburg airships to the planet Mars, and one back again.

More than 10,500 ocean~going ships will pass through the delta of the River Danube.

ODESSA
Kherson
Sarata
Karkinitsky Zaliv
Galati
Delta Dunării (Mouths of the Danube)
CRIMEA
ᴵANIA
Sevastopol   Yalta
Constanța
BLACK
Varna
ARIA
SEA
Burgas
Zonguldak   Sinop
ISTANBUL

Dall's porpoise will not sleep.

More people will probably be ADDED to the world population than existed on Earth when the Queen of England was seven (that was 1933).

I AM 7

More than three Million American women will have their nose changed...

1. $4,500
2. $7,000
3. $6,750
4. $5,800
5. $3,000
10 $5,500
11 $8,250
12

...by surgery.

Pesticides the weight of 113 Exxon Valdez supertankers will be spread over Europe (26 million tons).

Nurses will take care of enough English accident and emergency victims to populate the whole of western Europe.

Pairs of skylarks, endangered in built-up countries, will raise fledglings 30 million times in the grasslands of high-plateau Turkey.

HELP!

Winners of Britain's National Lottery...

Pairs of very rare white-tailed eagles

will try to nest 240 times in the British Isles.

...will take HOME enough money to give every child in the country an income of $184 a year.

Firefighters will rescue nearly one million Londoners locked out of their homes and offices ~ or locked in!

As in the past, Europe could lose an area of permanent meadows and pastures more than two times the size of Great Britain (207,473 sq mi during 1960~90).

100 million European women will get married.

3,000 Britons will have their portrait painted by Royal Society artists.

23

IN THE NEXT THREE CENTURIES...

Countless new varieties of

FLOWERS,

VEGETABLES,

FRUIT, AND

DOMESTIC

ANIMALS

will be bred for human and animal use.

Human settlements on the planet MARS will house more than 50,000 pioneers, with at least 9,000 children.*

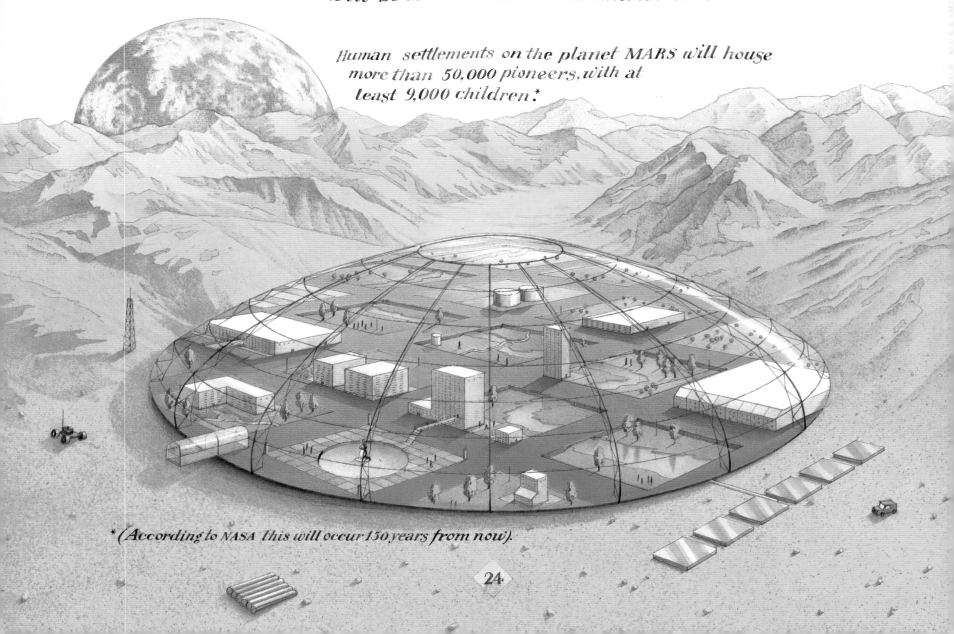

* (According to NASA this will occur 150 years from now).

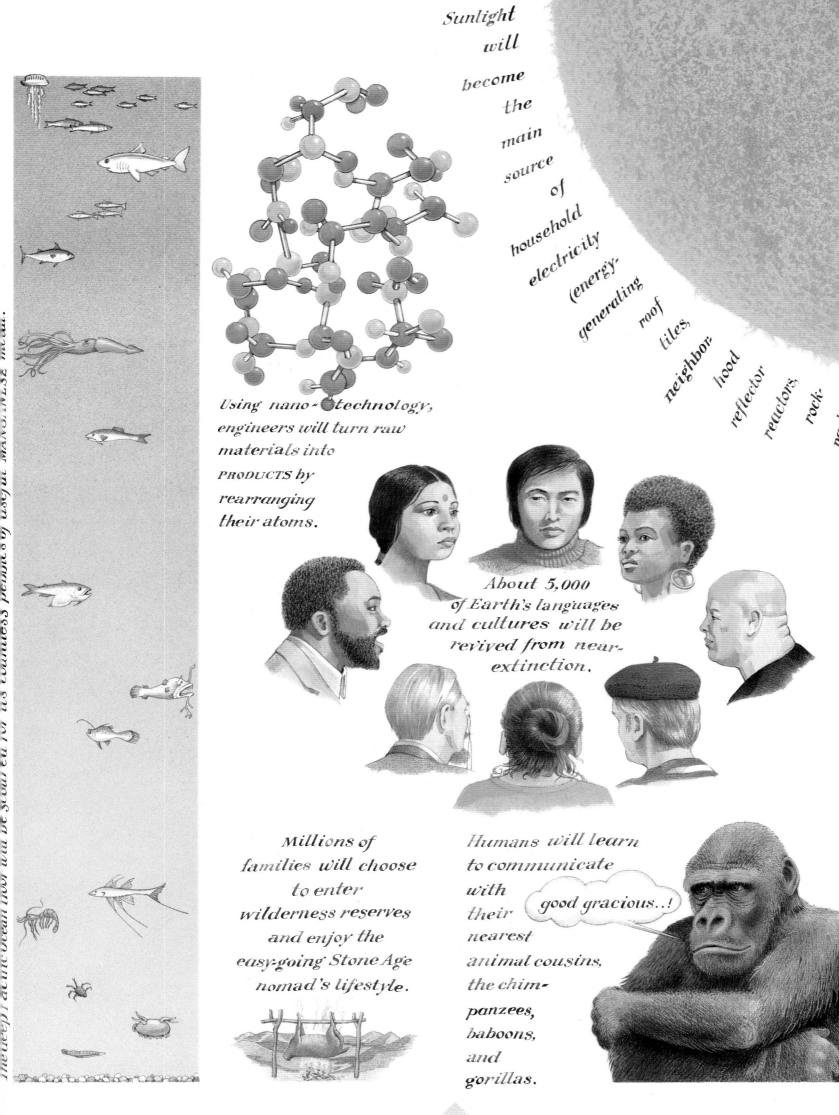

Sunlight will become the main source of household electricity (energy-generating roof tiles, neighborhood reflector reactors, rock-packed conservatories).

Using nano-technology, engineers will turn raw materials into PRODUCTS by rearranging their atoms.

About 5,000 of Earth's languages and cultures will be revived from near-extinction.

Millions of families will choose to enter wilderness reserves and enjoy the easy-going Stone Age nomad's lifestyle.

Humans will learn to communicate with their nearest animal cousins, the chimpanzees, baboons, and gorillas.

good gracious..!

25

In The Next Three Thousand Years...

A precious antique 1997 clock losing half a second per day will be only six days behind.

A hot-air balloon averaging 25 mph will have circled the planet 26,726 times.

Due to a worldwide ban on poaching, forests should be home to at least 32 million MORE wild Lynx (based on 10,775 trapped skins sold a year).

Based on present trends, the icy North... and South poles will have melted.

At current rates of global warming, the sea level will have risen between 16 and 59 feet, submerging most human settlements.

IN THE NEXT THREE MILLION YEARS...

The space probe
VOYAGER 2
will be leaving
our galaxy,
the Milky Way.

ACKNOWLEDGMENTS

All predictions are based on published official, trade, or reference sources.
Principal sources for statistics calculated for use in this book:
Parliamentary Debates, The Official Report (Hansard); Euromonitor plc; Panos
Institute; Demos; BP plc; Worldwatch Institute; MORI; Driver & Vehicle
Licensing Agency; U.S. Motor Vehicle Manufacturers' Association; United
Nations; U.S. Environmental Protection Agency; BBC News & Current Affairs;
Organization for Economic Cooperation & Development (OECD); New
Scientist; WARMER Bulletin; Whitakers Almanack; Hutchinson Encyclopedia;
The Cambridge Encyclopedia; The Guinness Book of Records; Eurostat,
Luxembourg; Statistical Abstract of the U.S.; Information Please Environmental
Almanac; U.S. Office of Management & Budget; Quid, Paris; British Airways
plc; The Pink Book, HMSO; Office of Population, Census, & Surveys (OPCS);
Canada Yearbook; Hutchinson Dictionary of Science; The Information Please
Almanac; Planet Gauge, The Real Facts Of Life; Planet Gauge 1993.

THE AUTHOR especially thanks the staff of Richmond-Upon-Thames
Reference Library.

INDEX